A Tale of Two Genies

Adapted by David Lewman
from the script "My Secret Genies" by Sindy Boveda Spackman

Illustrated by Dave Aikins

A GOLDEN BOOK • NEW YORK

randomhousekids.com
ISBN 978-0-553-52200-6
Printed in the United States of America
10 9 8 7 6 5 4 3 2

It was a beautiful morning in Zahramay Falls. Shine jumped out of bed. She couldn't wait to start her magical day.

"Woo-hoo!" she cheered. "Nahal, my sweet little tiger, do you know what today is?"

Nahal yawned.

"It's the day my twin sister, Shimmer, and I become genies!" Shine explained. "Well, more like genies-in-training. We finally get to grant wishes for our new friend! I'm so excited!"

The sleepy tiger crawled back under the covers.

"Come on!" Shine insisted. "Let's go wake up Shimmer!"

But Shimmer wasn't in her bed.
She wasn't under her vanity table.
She wasn't in her wardrobe closet.

"Where in the genie world did she go?" Shine asked. "Come on, Nahal. Let's look downstairs!"

In the living room, Shine spotted a collection of
pretty genie bottles. Suddenly, one began to shake.
Out popped Shimmer and her pet monkey, Tala!
    "What's with all the bottles, sis?" Shine asked.
    "I'm looking for the perfect one to give to our
new friend!" Shimmer explained.

Shine laughed. "We can't use just any old genie bottle! We have to make a new one with super-special ingredients!"

Shimmer clapped her hands. The genies' magic carpet appeared, and off they went to find their special ingredients.

The first thing the genies needed for their bottle was a flower petal.

But the genies couldn't pluck the petal. They had to have patience and wait for it to drop on its own.

"As genies-in-training," explained Shimmer, "we might make mistakes, so we're going to need a friend with a lot of patience!"

Finally, a blue petal fell from the flower,
and Shine placed it in a glittering box.

"One flower petal—check!" Shimmer
said. "Now for the fun part!"

With that, they flew off on their magic
carpet to find the next ingredient.

"Making sand castles at the beach sure is fun!" Shine said.

"Exactly!" Shimmer agreed. "And our new friend should be just as fun! That's why we'll be adding these fun beach memories to our genie bottle!"

Shimmer magically sent the whole sand castle into a jar. They had their second ingredient!

The genies hopped on their magic carpet and flew
into the air, right through a cloud.

"Whoa!" exclaimed Shine. "That cloud we just flew
through looks kind of like a heart!"

"That's right!" Shimmer said, grabbing some of the
cloud. "And we need a puff of this heart-shaped cloud
to match our friend's big, kind heart!"

...k at the palace, Shine put the
...dients into a bowl one by one.
...added a little glitter to make the
...e really sparkle!
...hine clapped her hands and
...ew, beautiful bottle appeared!

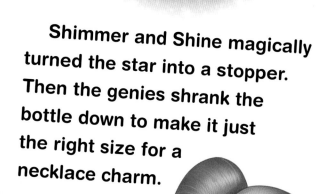

Shimmer and Shine magically
turned the star into a stopper.
Then the genies shrank the
bottle down to make it just
the right size for a
necklace charm.

It was perfect! But who would they give it to?

The magic carpet dove and landed in the ocean
with a splash! Shimmer and Shine used their carpet
like a surfboard to ride the waves.

"Surfing takes a lot of bravery," Shimmer said.
"And our new friend has to be brave, too."

Using an eyedropper, Shimmer collected the next
special ingredient: a little bit of their big ocean wave!

Leah laughed and hugged the genies. "I'm so lucky to have my very own genies!"

Shimmer said, "You're patient, fun, kindhearted, brave, and unique."

Shine added, "So *we're* the lucky ones to have *you*!"